The Lost Sketchbook

Written by Imam Baksh

Illustrated by Stacey Byer

Collins

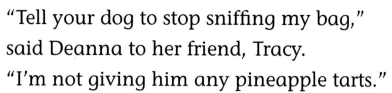

"Tell your dog to stop sniffing my bag,"
said Deanna to her friend, Tracy.
"I'm not giving him any pineapple tarts."

"You're in a bad mood,"
said Tracy. "Did your mother
say you can't have that
cricket bat you wanted?"

"She says I'm packing too much cricket into my brain and there's no room for other things."

That's when Deanna saw the sketchbook.

She picked it up and saw that it had no name on it. All the pages were blank.

Tracy said, "Isn't your mother always telling you to do more writing and drawing and dancing? You could fill this book with drawings and she'll see you do things besides cricket."

4

Deanna thought about the flower paintings her mother had on her walls. Deanna wanted to give her mother a pretty flower drawing.

She took a pencil from her school bag and pressed the tip to the first page. Her first few lines were shaky, but soon the shape of the flower started to appear. Deanna had never realised she was this good at drawing.

Then the sketchbook buzzed in Deanna's hands.

She dropped the book in surprise. And that knocked her flower out of the page!

"It fell out!" said Tracy.

"Wow! This book makes drawings become real," said Deanna.

The first thing Deanna did was draw
some money. But it just faded away before she
could get it out of the book.

"I wonder why it vanished?" said Tracy.

"So much for buying a bat," said Deanna.

Tracy borrowed the book and made a collar for Bruno, since he needed a new one.

"Well, that worked!" said Tracy.

Bruno loved the new collar.

Then Deanna decided to make a whole bunch
of flowers to give to her mother. As she drew,
the book kept buzzing louder and harder.

When Deanna pulled the flowers out of the sketchbook, she saw a swarm of huge bees behind them, flying straight at her.

"Bees," said Tracy. "They must be after the flowers. Quick, shut the book."

It was too late. The bees erupted out of
the sketchbook, knocking the girls over.

Yapping and yipping, Bruno chased the bees and they flew right into Mr Carter's fence. Right through the fence, in fact.

"We have to put the bees back in the book before they do any more damage,"
yelled Tracy.

"I'll draw a net and catch them with it,"
said Deanna.

"But bees are our friends," said Tracy. "They help plants grow food. We have to get them back to their home. Besides, they're too fast and strong to catch."

"OK," said Deanna. "I have an idea. But we need to get Bruno to stop chasing the bees. Call him over for some tarts."

"Hurry," shouted Tracy. "The bees are going to fly away soon. Who knows what they'll wreck next? They don't know their own strength."

"I'm drawing as fast as I can." Deanna tried to hurry and be careful at the same time, making the best drawing she had ever done in her life.

Tracy shouted at the bees to come back.
But they didn't seem to hear her.

Then Deanna held up her drawing. That got their attention. They turned and flew straight at her. She just hoped the bees would be able to get back into the book.

The bees loved the colourful scene that
Deanna had drawn for them.

They zoomed down and flew right into the sketchbook, breathing in the wonderful scents of all the new flowers they could see.

When they got to school that day,
Tracy borrowed the sketchbook and drew
a shiny new cricket bat as a reward for
Deanna helping the bees.

And Deanna put it to good use.
When she wasn't drawing, of course.

Sketchbook guide

by Deanna

1. Be careful. Sometimes other things are hidden behind what you draw.

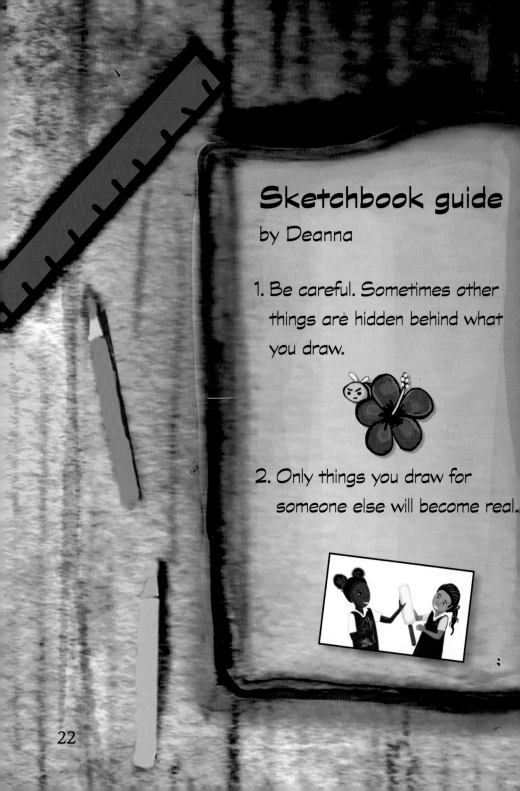

2. Only things you draw for someone else will become real.

3. Things you draw for yourself will
   fade away.

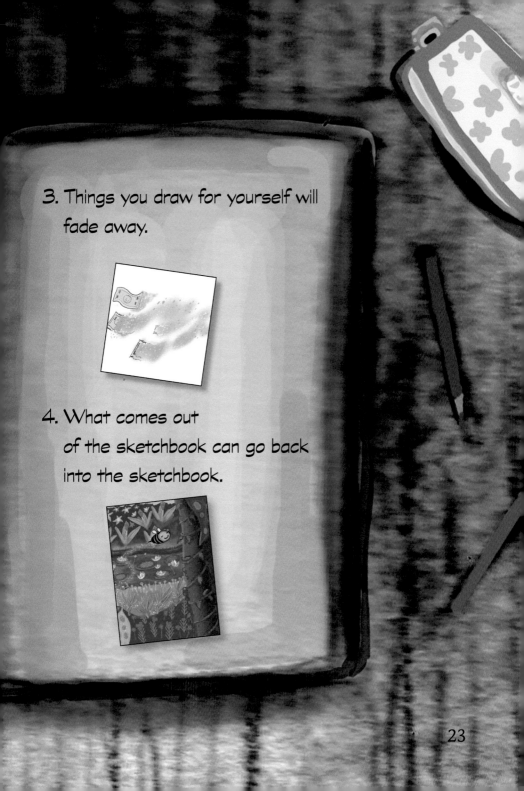

4. What comes out
   of the sketchbook can go back
   into the sketchbook.

 Ideas for reading

Written by Christine Whitney
Lecturer and Primary Literacy Consultant

Reading objectives:
- discuss the sequence of events in books
- make inferences on the basis of what is being said and done
- predict what might happen on the basis of what has been read so far

Spoken language objectives:
- ask relevant questions
- speculate, imagine and explore ideas through talk
- participate in discussions

Curriculum links: Science – Children should use the local environment throughout the year to explore and answer questions about animals and flowers in their habitat; Writing – write narratives about personal experiences and those of others, write for different purposes

Word count: 626 words

Interest words: pineapple tarts, sketchbook, erupted

Resources: paper, pencils and crayons for the children to make their own posters and sketchbooks

Build a context for reading

- Ask children if they know what a sketchbook is. Have they ever drawn in one? If they could draw anything, what would it be?
- Why could a sketchbook be lost? Ask children to discuss in pairs what might happen in a story about a lost sketchbook.
- What are the children's favourite desserts or puddings? Do they know what a fruit tart is? Have they ever eaten a pineapple tart?
- Ask children if they have ever read any stories about magical objects. Suggest that they tell the group about these stories.